Title: *Bearly in Between*
Subtitle: *Threesome MMF and Werebear Shifter Romance Story*

From the Author:
Thank you for purchasing this book.

Table of Contents

Title and Subtitle 1

Copyright 2

Bearly in Between 4

Description 4

Chapter 1 5

Chapter 2 16

Chapter 3 21

Chapter 4 24

Chapter 5 29

Chapter 6 33

Chapter 7 39

Bearly in Between
Description

Aaron Locke is the 30 year old handsome CEO of Locke industries, worth billions of dollars. He is known as a chronic womanizer but he has a scandalous secret which he has guarded all his life. He finds himself attracted to Arabella, his P.A only to find out that she's the wife of his gay lover.

Arabella Garcia is a 28-year-old beautiful and curvy bear-shifter who is married to her childhood best-friend in order to hide his sexuality. She receives the shock of her life when she finds her husband cheating on her with her crush.

Bernard Garcia is a 32-year-old bear-shifter who was forced by his parents to marry his childhood best-friend Arabella. He finally finds the love of his life in Aaron.

Will Bernard be willing to share his love with Ara and will Ara be able to forgive the two men she holds dear to her heart?

Chapter 1

"Ara," Aaron called as he tapped Ara bringing her back to reality.

"We are here," Aaron stated looking at Arabella in concern.

Ara turned to look outside the window and noticed that his car was actually packed in front of the restaurant.

"I'm so sorry," Ara apologized for the tenth time that day. Mentally slapping herself for being absent minded and embarrassing herself in front of her boss again.

Aaron frowned knowing fully well that something was bothering her but decided not to probe further. He would bring that up later.

"'It's ok," he said as he leaned over and removed her seat belt keeping an eye on her as he did so.

Her heart fluttered as she got lost in his forest green eyes.

"Get down, Ara." He withdrew away from her and smiled, satisfied that he had such an effect on her.

"Yeah." She clumsily got out of the car feeling stupid for having been caught staring.

He led the way into the restaurant while she followed.

"Good evening, Mr. Locke." A tall blonde woman dressed in a waitress uniform greeted him.

He smiled flashing his perfect white teeth which made her blush.

"Please follow me to your private booth," said the Waitress.

"Ok," Aaron replied smiling at the woman who was clearly flirting with him.

Any other day he would have had his way with her but he couldn't afford to flirt back especially with Ara there. It just wasn't right.

They were led to the private booth while Aaron thanked the waitress who slipped a paper into his hand which most probably contained her number.

"What would you like to order?" the waitress asked her eyes fixed on Aaron.

It didn't skip Ara's attention that the Waitress had not acknowledged her for one second. She was too engrossed in flirting with Aaron to notice her.

Arabella rolled her eyes at the scene in front of her though it didn't come as a surprise to her.

Aaron was hot and handsome. He always made it to the list of the most sought after bachelors in America who had girls flaunting themselves at him.

He could get any girl at the snap of his finger but she always wondered why he couldn't just settle with one.

Aaron scanned the Restaurant's Menu for a few seconds before placing it back on the table.

"Get me an oven roasted Gulf fish fisherman's style with red wine."

"What about you, Ara?"

Ara forced a smile. "I will take the same order as yours."

She was not hungry. She just didn't want Aaron to ask her more questions.

"Ok," the waitress nodded, still not taking her eyes off Aaron who was beginning to look uncomfortable. She winked at him and wiggled her hips as she walked by, hoping he was watching her.

However, his eyes were fixed on Ara who was trying to stifle a laugh.

"What's funny?" he asked a hint of a smile on his face.

She looked so adorable trying not to laugh and he really wanted to know the reason behind her laughter. So he can do it again just to see her face light up.

"I'm just laughing at her antics. She is willing to lose her job for you and you didn't even spare her a glance."

"How could I when I have someone more precious in front of me?" he blurted out but didn't regret it on seeing her blush and shift on her chair.

She looked around the private booth hoping for a distraction to calm her nerves. She looked back at him only to find his gaze still on her.

She cleared her throat in an attempt to ease the tension and asked "When is the Client going to get here?"

He started chuckling.

"What did I say that is so funny?" Ara thought.

"Why are you laughing, sir?"

He stops chuckling and leaned on the table, his gaze now serious.

"I've told you countless times that you shouldn't call me sir outside the office."

Ara bit her lip. "I'm sorry, Aaron."

"Good." He smiled, satisfied by her answer.

"You still haven't answered my question. Where is the client that we are supposed to meet here?"

He starts chuckling again and shook his head. "Oh! Ara, you are so innocent."

"There's no client. I brought you here so we could talk."

She opened her mouth in shock and closed it back "Why?"

"I have noticed that you have been distracted at work lately. I keep on asking you what's wrong but you keep evading the subject."

Ara rolled her eyes, offended that he had tricked her. "That's because I don't want to talk about it."

He sighed and clasped his hands together.

" Ara, I thought we'd passed this stage. I confided in you about my personal issues something I've never done before. I thought we are friends."

Ara sighed. "Yes, we are."

"Then what is stopping you from confiding in me, your friend?"

Seeing that she remained silent, he continued.

"I respect your choice but I can see that there's something eating you up and you really need to vent it out. Mind you I'm a good listener." He flashed his pearly white teeth.

Ara shook her head in disapproval. "I can't tell you. It's not appropriate."

"Is it about your husband?" he asked, catching her off guard. The look on her face and the fact that she made no effort to deny it confirmed Aaron's suspicions.

"How... how did you know? Is it that obvious?" Ara asked.

"I have my ways but that's not important right now."

He placed his hand on hers.

"Talk to me, your secret is safe with me."

"It's not that important." Ara dismissed. She wasn't used to being vulnerable especially in front of her Boss.

He rolled his eyes at her and crossed his arms. "It's important enough for you to be distracted at work and end up spilling hot coffee all over me."

She bit her lip recalling the mistake she had made earlier that day at the office.

She had been filling his cup with coffee but was lost in thoughts that she didn't notice that the cup was full until Aaron shouted and she saw that it had stained his suit.

"I told you to see me as your friend outside the company. You can trust me with that. Like I said your secret is safe with me." He assured placing his hand on yours.

She sighed knowing he was right. She really needed someone to confide in but she had no friends here. All her relatives were still primitive preferring not to mingle with humans. She also couldn't confide in them without being judged.

"It's just... I don't know... it might not be true... I just feel like my husband is cheating on me."

"What? Why would you think that?" he asked in surprise. He clearly wasn't expecting that.

"I've been seeing the signs and a lady is 80-percent right when she suspects that her man is cheating on her."

"But you can't be so sure."

"I know but I just can't help feeling this way," Ara muttered sadly.

His heart hurt seeing her so vulnerable. He squeezed her hand softly making her look up at him.

"If he's really cheating on you then he's nothing but a loser."

"You are an impeccable woman, Ara, any man would be lucky to have you."

"Nah, you are just saying that just to make me feel better." Ara dismissed smiling.

He lifted her hand up and kissed it affectionately keeping his eyes on her.

"I meant every word."

Her heart fluttered at the gesture and she wondered how his lips would feel on hers.

As soon as the thought appeared, she quickly withdrew her hand away from his, wondering why she had such improper thoughts about him.

Though, she couldn't blame herself entirely. He was every woman's dream and her secret crush but he didn't have to know that.

It was wrong, totally wrong to feel that way about him as a married woman but she couldn't help it. That's why she always minimized their physical contacts, afraid that she would fall in deep with no going back.

She cleared her throat in order to get rid of the awkwardness in the air.

It was then the waitress arrived with their orders.

Ara had never been so happy to see the waitress again. She had saved her from the obvious tension in the room.

The waitress left after delivering their orders.

Ara cleared his throat once again. "We should probably start eating."

"Yeah, you are right," said Aaron his eyes never leaving Ara.

They ate their food in silence each of them wondering how to break the awkwardness in the air.

He was getting irritated with the silence.

"I'm sorry for making you uncomfortable," Aaron apologized while Ara looked up from her meal and smiled.

"You didn't."

"I clearly did." He watched her lips as she ate.

A little stain was by her lips and he wondered how it would feel to brush his fingers against her lips.

Feeling his gaze on her, she looked up from her meal.

"Ara, you got a little uh- something here." He gestured to her lip.

"Oh!" she muttered and licked the side of her lip.

"Damn, she would be the death of me." He thought as he watched her try to lick the stain off with no idea what it was doing to him.

"Is it gone?" she innocently asked a flustered Aaron.

Aaron shook his head and she groaned. He sighed and left his seat to sit beside her.

Ara's heart quickened at the proximity. She couldn't stand being close to him with those forest green eyes boring into her brown orbs.

"Here," he said as he brought his thumb to the side of her upper lip, his hand slightly gracing her lips.

He marveled at how soft they were and with just a wipe, the stain was gone but his thumb stayed put and his eyes stayed glued on her lips wondering how it would feel to kiss them.

He looked up to meet her eye but found them staring at his lips with as much longing as his own. He needed no further clue to know that she wanted this as much as him.

Her eyes stayed glued to his lips watching as his tongue darted out to wet pink lips.

Her eyes snapped up immediately hoping that she hadn't been caught but the look in his eyes told her that she had been caught.

Before she could bring herself to say something, Aaron had planted her lips on her.

He kissed her sweetly and softly before he pulled away to meet her gaze.

His heart was beating frantically against his chest. He so bad wanted to kiss her again but he needed to know that she wanted it as much as him.

"Ara," he whispered bringing her back to reality.

"Yes?" she managed to say hoping that she didn't sound too nervous.

"Was that... was that ok? Can I kiss you again?" he asked slowly hoping that he had not scared her away.

She didn't know what did it for her. Was it the look of hope in his eyes or the fact that she wanted to kiss him again?

The next thing she knew, she had kissed him.

He froze in shock at her action but quickly recovered and kissed her back harder. She reached up and wrapped her hands around the back of his neck pulling him closer.

Butterflies exploded in her chest as he slipped his tongue into her mouth relishing in the taste of her. She moaned when she felt his hand grip her hips.

He needed to have her closer to him. No woman had made him hard with just a kiss.

He had kissed so many girls before her but they paled in comparison.

He was dying to have her close and bury himself in her. Having her scream his name all night as he fucked her senseless.

She gasped as he felt his hand move to her open thigh rubbing slowly. Then her eyes snapped open bringing her back to reality.

She was kissing her boss. She was kissing Aaron in the restaurant. She was kissing another man when she was a married woman. She was a married woman!

She quickly pushed him away as reality dawned on her.

He nearly whined as she broke the kiss but stopped on seeing the look on her face.

Her eyes were watery as if on the verge of tears. Her hand moved to cover her swollen lips as she stifled a cry.

He tried to reach for her but she stood up shaking her head. "Don't touch me!" she managed to say her voice breaking.

She quickly grabbed her purse and ran out of the restaurant.

"Shit," Aaron cursed as he ran after her.

He found her on the street waving various cabs down as they passed. He brushed his hand through his hair and walked to her, grabbing her hand to make her face him.

"Don't touch me!" she yelled this time.

"Ara, I'm sorry," he apologized sincerely. He shouldn't have put her in a vulnerable position. He was sorry for that but he wasn't sorry for kissing her.

He would give anything to kiss those lips again but it wasn't right. She was a married woman and he had to respect that.

"I'm really sorry."

"No, you are not. You clearly wanted it."

He ran his hands through his hair again wondering what to say to her.

"This shouldn't have happened. It should never have happened. This is all my fault. I shouldn't have followed you to this stupid dinner. I shouldn't have allowed you to take advantage of me."

He frowned not believing his ears. "I took advantage of you?"

He let out a laugh devoid of humour "You clearly wanted it. I asked for your consent and what did you do, you kissed me back."

Her heart sank as she took in his words. He was right. She had entertained him. It was her fault. She was the married one. She should have had more control over her feelings.

"Just leave me alone." She pleaded eager to leave the premises. The close proximity between them was not helping her mental state at the moment.

He gave her an incredulous look. "I can't just leave you alone in the middle of nowhere."

"Yes, you can. Now please let me go."

She looked down at his hold on her arm but he didn't budge.

"No, let me drive you home." He protested ignoring her plea.

"Are you crazy? Do you really expect me to let you drive me home after what happened between us?"

He knew she was right but he couldn't just leave her all by herself.

"Please leave me alone. I'm begging you," she pleaded.

The desperation in her voice tugged at his heart and he let her go.

He walked back to where his car was parked and waited until she got inside a cab.

He really wanted to follow her home but he realised how foolish that would be. He had done enough damage already.

Chapter 2

She paused on her way to the front door when she spotted her husband's car in the garage.

He's home early. She thought to herself.

Normally, she would be happy because it was a rare occurrence for him to be home before her but the guilt in her wasn't eager to see him just yet.

She felt like a hypocrite for suspecting him to be cheating when she was doing the same.

Her hand reached for the doorknob and she sighed.

She mustered up courage and opened the door confirming her suspicions.

There he was seated on the sofa in the living room watching the news when his eyes met hers as she entered.

His face broke into a wide grin as he jumped out of the sofa and rushed towards her, enveloping her in an embrace.

She froze at his sudden action wondering why he was so happy.

Bernard frowned when Ara refused to hug him back. He slowly released her from his embrace to look at her.

"What's wrong?" he asked brushing a strand of hair that was blocking her vision away.

She finally managed to find her voice. "Good evening, Darling." She greeted while he just gave her a questioning look.

"That doesn't answer my question."

She shrugged out of his hold and made her way to the kitchen.

Afraid that he would see right through her after all, he was her best-friend. He knew everything about her.

"Nothing is wrong with me," she answered as she opened the fridge and took out a chilled bottled water and downed the contents into a glass cup.

"Are you sure? You don't look fine to me," he asked worriedly.

She looked to be hiding something from him and it scared him because Ara never hid any secrets from him. He was her confidante.

Yeah right. You don't want her to hide things from you but you are doing the same to her, his subconscious said to him making him feel guilty and brush the thought way.

"I said I'm fine!" she snapped startling him.

She looked up to meet his gaze. He looked offended and she couldn't blame him.

She brought the cup to her lips and sipped her water in order to calm her nerves.

"Why are you home late?" he asked all of a sudden as he made his way to the kitchen to stand beside her.

She almost spat out the water she was drinking at his question.

Feeling his gaze on her, she placed the cup back on the kitchen cabinet and took a deep breath before she answered.

"I was at a business meeting with my boss." Technically she wasn't lying. She really thought it would be a business meeting until Aaron told her the truth.

"A business meeting where you kiss your boss," her subconscious asked her making her guilt to return ten folds.

"I... I have to freshen up. Good night." She smiled at him and scurried off to the bathroom to avoid his questioning gaze.

Bernard leaned against the kitchen cabinet as he watched her leave for their room.

He couldn't blame her for acting cold to him when he had been doing the exact same thing for the past for four months.

He took a sip from her abandoned cup and sighed.

Ever since he had met Aaron at the pub, he had been complete.

They had hooked up and at first he thought what he felt for him was just a fluke but when he couldn't help going back to him, he knew it wasn't just a fluke.

He had found his soulmate.

His bear purred every time he saw Aaron. He sighed as felt himself harden at the thought of Aaron.

All his life, he had been nothing but a good son to his parents even to the point of hiding his sexuality because it wasn't acceptable for bear-shifters to be gay. They were supposed to end up with their soul-mate, a female bear-shifter.

He didn't mean to cheat on Ara but theirs was not a normal marriage. Gay bears were an abomination and she saved his family reputation by marrying him.

She had always been in love with him since they were kids but he couldn't return that love no matter how much he tried to. He just couldn't do it.

He loved her but he was not in love with her.

How would he break it to her that he had defiled their marriage vows? She deserved to know but he couldn't bear to break her heart. She was too dear to him.

He made his way into their room and sat down on the bed. There was no going back. He would tell her the truth now. No matter how hard it would be. She deserved to know.

He heard the sound of the shower stopping and her footsteps as she made her way into the room wrapped in a white robe.

She gasped in shock on seeing him there.

"Bernard?"

He smiled at her. "I figured that it's time for me to retire to bed too."

He gestured to her to sit on his laps while she looked at him in question.

"Please."

She sighed and sat on his laps wrapping her hands round his neck while he rocked her back and forth as if she was a baby.

"I'm sorry," he muttered while she looked at him confused.

"I'm sorry for the way I've been acting for the past few months. I shouldn't have treated you coldly."

Ever since he had started cheating on her with Aaron, he had been cold to her just to hide his guilt.

She shook her head and placed her finger on his lip to cut him off.

"Shh... I should have been more understanding."

He shook his head not agreeing with her. "No you don't get it Ara, I... I..."

He groaned. *Why is it so hard to say?* he thought to himself.

"I-"

She cut him off and kissed him.

She moaned in pleasure as she explored his mouth. She needed him so bad.

She gripped the collar of his chest pulling him closer. She needed him so bad.

It's been so long since they had had sex. Exactly five months and she couldn't stand it anymore.

She grinded against him, making him groan against her mouth.

She stood up and let her robe slip off her body revealing her naked tanned curvy body. She climbed unto his lap again and whispered in his ear.

"Make love to me."

He froze and gently pushed her away.

"I can't. I can't do it."

She pulled away slightly to look at his face and frowned "You can't?"

He avoided her gaze. "Yes, I'm sorry."

"I'm just not in the mood. Let's just go back to sleep."

The disappointed look on her face told him he had messed up once again but how could he sleep with her when Aaron was on his mind. He couldn't sleep with her and risk moaning Aaron's name.

He couldn't do that to her. It was not fair to her.

She slowly got out of his lap, picked up her robe from the floor and wore it.

He reached for her hand. "Ara, I'm sorry."

"it's ok. It's fine." She didn't look at him. She was disappointed. He had rejected her once again.

She climbed onto bed and slipped the covers over her.

He knew it wasn't fine. She was mad at him. So mad!

He ran his hand through his blonde hair in frustration. He didn't know how he could make it up to her but he knew it was better if he left her alone for a while so he left for the guest room.

Chapter 3

She released a shaky breath as someone's fingers pushed in and out of her in an unrelenting tempo.

Pleasure built between her legs as they trembled causing her to release a soft moan.

"Faster." She gasped loudly arching her back wanting to feel the fingers inside her the more.

The person increased the pace, slamming his fingers in and out of her, circling her clit bringing her closer to her release.

Her panting ceased for a moment and she slowly opened her eyes to behold familiar forest green eyes staring down at her.

"Aaron?" she asked in shock.

He smirked. "The one and only."

He gave her one last thrust and she came all over his fingers.

"Ara."

She felt someone tap her.

"Ara."

Ara's eyes snapped open as she took in her surroundings. She sat up when she saw Bernard was staring down at her in concern.

"Are you ok?" he asked.

She managed to nod wiping the sweat on her forehead with her palm.

She had just had a wet dream about her boss, Aaron. It was a miracle that she didn't moan out his name. It would have been embarrassing.

"You are late for work."

She quickly glanced at the wall clock the memories of the kiss she shared with Aaron coming back to her like a vengeance.

No, I can't go to work. I just had a wet dream about him. How can I handle working with him when I can't even resist him? The right thing to do as a married woman is to resign and that's what I'm going to do. She thought to herself.

"My boss gave me a morning break because of the late night meeting we had yesterday," she lied.

She couldn't bring herself to tell him just yet that she was resigning because that would prompt a lot of questions that she wasn't ready to answer.

"Your boss is so nice," Bernard said as he fixed his apron.

If only you knew. She thought to herself.

"By the way, breakfast is ready. Should I bring it here or you will come down to eat?" he asked a flustered Ara.

"I will come down to eat it. Right now I need to freshen up." she replied wanting some time alone to herself to gather her thoughts.

He smiled and pecked her on the lips before leaving the room.

As soon as he left, she reached under the blanket to her night robe and felt her wetness.

She didn't just come in her dream but in real life too.

She scurried off the bed and headed for the bathroom in need for a cold shower. She would have to draft the resignation letter immediately for her own sanity.

Bernard removed his apron and placed it on the kitchen cabinet.

He brushed his hand through his hair as he remembered how Ara writhed on the bed.

He knew she had a wet dream especially after he denied her sex last night. He would have to make it up to her and look for a way to get Aaron out of his system.

It wasn't fair to Ara at all.

Chapter 4

Aaron was restless as he paced his office waiting for the one person he was dying to see.

He took a glance at his wristwatch which read 12:30 pm and groaned.

"How could she not report to work?" he asked himself as he loosened his tie. He threw the tie across the room not caring where it landed.

A knock came on the door and he yelled, "What?"

The door opened to reveal a gorgeous Arabella who was dressed in a black crew-neck sweater with a black leather mini dress which hugged her hourglass shape which made his mouth dry up.

"How dare she look so good? How am I supposed to keep my hands to myself with her dressed like this?" he thought to himself.

He shook his dirty thoughts away and frowned, "You are late."

He went back to his seat and sat down folding his arms trying to look like he was furious with her when it was the exact opposite.

He was going to act like the boss she wanted.

She didn't say anything. She just made her way to his table and handed him a white envelope.

He stared at the envelope in confusion.

"What is this?" he asked as he collected the envelope.

"That's my resignation letter."

"What!" he exclaimed in shock. He couldn't have possibly heard her right.

She rolled her eyes. "You heard me."

"Why are you resigning? It doesn't make sense."

He stood up and walked towards her.

"If this is about what happened last night, I'm sorry. It won't happen again."

"I admit I crossed my boundaries but please don't leave me." He pleaded.

The sincerity behind his words melted her heart and the fact that he was just few feet away from her didn't help matters.

The first two buttons of his white shirt were unbuttoned revealing smooth tan skin. His white shirt fitted him perfectly, hugging his abs.

She wondered how it would feel to run her hands over them. Then she remembered her dream, the way he was...

She felt herself getting wet at the memory.

"This is the right thing to do," she managed to say ignoring her improper thoughts.

He closed the space between them and traced his thumb from her cheek to her lips.

"But why does it feel so right?" he whispered, his hot breath fanning her face.

He didn't give her time to digest what was going on before he grabbed her neck, pulling her closer and kissing her.

It didn't take long for her to start to struggle against him but he didn't budge deepening the kiss.

She felt him moving her towards the table until her butt sat on it.

She couldn't resist anymore and she kissed him back with as much ferocity, brushing her hands through his hair.

His free hand started trailing up her slightly parted thighs until he reached her soaked panties. She was wet for him making him smirk.

His hand rubbed her wet pussy through her thong making her let out a soft moan.

He pulled out of the kiss and rested his forehead against hers "You are so wet for me." He smiled as his fingers pushed her thong out of the way rubbing her the more.

She threw her head back moaning. It's been so long since she had been touched like this. It had been so-so long so it was understandable that her body was betraying her.

Before she could make a final decision on whether she should follow her brain or not, he had already slipped his fingers into her wet cunt making her let out a loud moan, arching her back wanting him to push into her the more.

"Do you want this?" he asked as he withdrew his finger and pinched at her swollen clit, teasingly rubbing his fingers on her outer lips.

Her brain was telling her to push him away but her body stayed put letting him explore her secret haven.

"Yes," she whispered. It was barely a whisper but he heard her alright.

"Yes what?" he asked as he slipped one finger into her again circling it.

"Yes, I want it," she whimpered.

He smiled happy and pushed two more fingers into her making her cry out in pleasure.

He began to push his fingers in and out of her, thrusting into her harder and faster. He caught her whimpers with a deep kiss.

She was writhing against him and he could feel himself getting hard by her motion.

His cock was straining out of his trousers begging to be released. Damn, he wanted to fuck her on the table right there but he couldn't do it.

He didn't want their first time to be over the table. She was special. She was his Ara, not some random fling.

He sped up his swirls around her clit making her lean against him.

Not long after, she was climaxing, bucking hard as she cried out, squirting and cumming all over his fingers.

He withdrew his fingers slowly and licked it clean watching her.

It was then it dawned on her that she had just been fingered by another man other than her husband. She felt like a slut.

She quickly pulled her skirt down and walked away from him as if he was some plague.

"Oh my God, What have I done?" she asked herself.

He chuckled. "You mean what have we done?"

She rolled her eyes and glared at him.

"Hey, there's no need to feel bad. I mean we both wanted this. We are both adults who clearly wanted this."

"But this is wrong."

"Says the woman whose husband is probably somewhere fucking a bitch's brain out and you are here denying yourself pleasure."

"That still doesn't make what we did, right."

"The sooner you accept that you want me as much as I want you, the better for you cause if you think I'm going let you go, you must be joking."

She shook her head. "I'm not going to stand here and let you ruin my marriage, Goodbye forever, Mr. Locke."

She didn't spear him a second glance before she dashed out of his office banging the door after her.

He would be damned to let her go.

Ever since, she had walked into his into his office a year ago looking for work. He had been entranced with her.

He wanted to bed her bad but when he found out that she was married, he had to keep his feelings in check.

He didn't mess with married women but as he got to know her better, he realised that he wasn't just interested in sleeping with her, he wanted to be with her and the only person he had ever felt that way for was Bernard. How would Bernard take this news?

He felt his member harden at the thought of Bernard. He really needed him right now.

He picked up his phone from the table and dialed Bernard's number.

Chapter 5

Aaron parked his Tesla in front of Bernard's House and got out slamming the door after him.

He stood beside his car as he admired the modest house. He had always wondered why Bernard never wanted him to know where he lived.

Aaron had thought he was living in a rugged neighborhood but when the private investigator he hired had sent the pictures to him, it was then he knew there was something else Bernard was trying to hide from him.

He observed his surroundings for a while before he pressed the doorbell.

Bernard was in the kitchen washing the dishes when he heard the sound of the doorbell.

He frowned wondering who it could be since he wasn't expecting any visitor and neither was Ara after all she was visiting her Mum in Placerville and wouldn't be back till the next day.

He sighed and cleaned his hands with the hand towel, then headed for the front door. He hesitated a little and opened it only to receive the shock of his life.

There standing on the doorstep was Aaron, looking as handsome as ever in a casual white shirt and dark blue jeans matched with blue sneakers. Bernard gulped as he stared at the love of his life.

Aaron broke into a wide grin and held out his arms for a hug "Surprise."

Bernard looked behind Aaron in panic. "What are you doing here?"

Aaron smiled. "To see you." he said it as if it was the most obvious thing in the world.

"But you can't be here!"

Aaron closed the space between them pressing his chest against Bernard's own.

"Why not?" he whispered in his ear and bit it softly.

Bernard felt his cock start to harden in his pants but he ignored it and took a step back. He couldn't allow Aaron to enter into his house and find out he was married this way.

Aaron pushed Bernard out of the way and entered the room with Bernard following after.

"You have to leave now!" Bernard tried to appear firm ignoring Aaron's intense gaze.

"Do you really want me to leave?" Aaron asked as he gripped the back of Bernard's head and kissed him, grinding his hard length against his.

Bernard moaned kissing Aaron back passionately. He moaned in protest when Aaron pulled away.

"Take me to your room."

It was a command that he couldn't resist. He captured Aaron's lips devouring it like he couldn't let go as he led him down the hall way to his room.

They grabbed at each other's clothes till they were naked. Aaron laid Bernard on the bed, their tongues still exploring each other.

Aaron reached down and grabbed Bernard's cock stroking it, earning a groan from Bernard.

"I missed you," Aaron said as he squeezed Bernard's cock extra hard making him whimper.

They relished at the skin to skin contact, their cocks rubbing against each other. They continued to pump each other, groans and moans filling the room.

"I need you," whispered Bernard.

Aaron grinned and withdrew away from him.

"Lay face down," he commanded Bernard who eagerly obeyed after grabbing a jar of Vaseline on the bed side table and handed it to a pleased Aaron.

Aaron took a handful of the Vaseline and rubbed it all over his cock. He rubbed his hardened member on Bernard's butt, guiding his slippery cock towards his tight hole.

He placed the head of his thick cock to Bernard's hole and pushed in slowly till he could go no further.

"Harder," Bernard mumbled while Aaron retreated a little before thrusting in, harder and faster.

"You feel so damn good!" Aaron hissed, his voice almost lost in pleasure. He grabbed both of Bernard's hands with his own and laid his chest on his back as his cock slid in and out of the other man smoothly.

Aaron closed his eyes imagining Ara under him as he fucked her in different positions while she cries out his name.

He grunted as he increased his strokes, aggressively fucking the man under him.

"I'm gonna cum soon. Come on." Bernard growled.

"Oh god," moaned Aaron quickening his pace, even more.

The sound of a door creaking open made him freeze.

"Is there anybody else here?" he asked Bernard.

"No, it's probably the breeze. Just don't stop," he answered with his eyes closed in ecstasy.

"Cum!" he demanded increasing his pace even more, making Bernard let out a strangled moan and trembled shouting Aaron's name as he came, spurting onto the sheets below him.

Unable to hold it back any longer, Aaron gripped Bernard's palm and spilled his seeds into his ass.

Panting, he lay beside Bernard exhausted trying to catch his breath.

He stared at the spent man beside him and muttered, "I love you, Bernard."

He traced his fingers through his hair while Bernard whispered, "I love you too."

He was about to kiss Bernard when they heard a loud gasp and saw Ara leaning against the door.

Chapter 6

She brought her hand to her mouth at the scene in front of her. She had entered the house only to hear loud groans and moans.

She decided to check for herself only to see Aaron and her husband naked in an intimate position. It didn't take her too long to put two and two together and discover that they had sex.

Heartbroken and feeling betrayed, she ran out of the room to the parlor sinking to the floor as she tried to make sense of what she just saw.

"Shit!" Bernard cursed as he climbed out of bed and quickly slipped his boxers on.

"What is going on? Why is she here?"

"'She's my wife!" Bernard blurted out not bothering to hide the truth anymore.

"What!" Aaron was in shock as he sat up on the bed.

"Yeah, I have to go."

He didn't wait for Aaron's answer before he darted out of the room to see Ara on the floor staring into space.

He sat beside her and sighed.

"I know that there's nothing I'm going to say that would fix this but-"

She turned to look at him with tear-stricken eyes cutting him off. "I knew you were cheating on me. I was ok with it but I didn't expect it to be with my boss." Her voice broke as she tried to blink her tears away.

"I didn't know he was your boss until I had fallen deep. Believe me I didn't want to hurt you."

"But you did. You still did. You had the guts to do it on our matrimonial bed." She paused to catch her breath and continued. "How many times have you done this on that same bed that we sleep on? Don't you have any shame?"

"Listen, Ara, I didn't mean to... it just so happened that..."

"That what?" she snapped.

The sound of footsteps interrupted their conversation and they looked up just in time to see Aaron walk into the room fully dressed.

Ara stood up and stomped toward him, landing a slap on his face.

"How could you?"

Aaron rubbed his cheek and glanced towards Bernard who was avoiding his gaze in guilt.

"Ara!"

"Don't you dare call my name! Was this your plan all along? You were using me the same way you used him?"

"No, no, you are getting this all wrong. I didn't know he was your husband," Aaron tried to clarify to a fuming Ara.

"Óh! So you found out just now!"

"That's exactly what happened." He nodded hoping that she would believe him. He knew Bernard was hiding something. He just wasn't expecting it to be this. Why of all women did he have to be married to Ara.

She scoffed, rolling her eyes, not believing him one bit.

Bernard stood up and sighed. "He's right. I didn't tell him that I was married. Even when I found out that you worked for him, I still didn't tell him. And I'm sorry for that, Aaron. I'm really sorry." He apologized looking down at the floor with red cheeks.

Ara ran her hands through her hair and exhaled "How long has this been going on?" she asked no one in particular.

"Four... four months," Bryan stammered knowing now that she was never going to forgive him. He had been distant to her for those four months.

She closed her eyes and asked the question that had been plaguing her mind since she caught them in the act. "Do you love him?"

He hesitated a little wondering how he could lessen the hurt she was going through because of him but he knew he had already hurt her enough. There was no going back from here.

"Yes, I love him."

Her heart broke at his confession. Bernard was her first everything, her first love, the first man who made love to her. The only man she had sworn that she would ever love.

It was hard to grasp that he was in love with someone else, not just someone else but her boss, the same person she was starting to fall for.

Unable to stand the tension in the room and wanting some alone time to himself to understand the situation, Aaron announced.

"I will just go." He didn't wait for any answer. He made to leave but Ara held his hand preventing him from leaving.

He turned to look at her.

"Nobody is leaving here until we settle this," she said with an air of finality looking at the two men in front of her.

She turned to look at Aaron who had a questioning look on his face and asked, "Do you love him too?"

He wasn't expecting that question at all. Neither did she expect that she would stop him from leaving. He looked at Bernard who was already staring at him in anticipation waiting for him to admit the truth.

"I do," he finally replied avoiding Ara's gaze.

She suddenly started clapping and let out a laugh devoid of humor. "Bravo, the great Aaron Locke is in love. Let's see how long that would last."

She moved to stand beside Bernard who was already feeling anxious wondering what she was up to.

"Bernard, why don't you show your love who you really are? Don't you want to see if he really loves you?"

He could sense the mockery in her voice. He refused to believe she was suggesting that. She couldn't possibly be suggesting what he thought she was suggesting.

"I don't know what you are talking about." He prayed that his suspicions wouldn't come true.

She scoffed "Oh! Please Bernard, aren't you tired of the lies? Don't you want to know if his feelings are true?"

Aaron frowned obviously confused. "'What is going on here?"

"Good question," Ara smiled. "Bernard here has one more secret he is hiding from you."

Aaron turned his gaze to an anxious looking Bernard. "Bernard, is this true?"

Bernard remained silent wishing that the ground would just swallow him up right there.

"He won't be able to tell you but I will show you."

She reached behind her back and zipped down her dress and slipped out of it.

Aaron's confused gaze turned to that of shock as he took in her appearance. She was now semi-naked with a pink c-cup bra and matching lace panties.

He could see through her panties that she was totally bare. He felt himself harden at the mesmerizing sight in front of him.

He closed his eyes and shook his head willing the image away. This was not the right time.

"What the hell are you doing?" Bernard asked Ara who rolled her eyes.

"What you should have done a long time ago before you got yourself in this mess."

Then she shifted into a gorgeous brown bear with red highlights, startling Aaron who took several steps back in disbelief until his back hit the wall.

"What...what is going on here?" he asked a Bewildered Bernard who was still finding it hard to believe that Ara had just shifted in front of Aaron.

"What the hell is that thing?" he asked again pointing to the brown bear whose eyes were fixed on him.

"That's Ara."

Aaron's eyes widened as he took in the information. That couldn't be Ara. It wasn't possible. Yes, she was right there before this thing came out. It just couldn't be.

"She's a werebear, so am I." Bernard finally admitted changing into a brown bear as well.

"This has to be a dream. You must be kidding me."

Aaron felt dizzy as if he was about to faint.

Unable to handle the scene in front of him, he rushed out of the room.

He ran till he got to his car panting as he leaned against it.

"I must be going crazy," he said to himself as he tried to catch his breath. "This can't be real."

He managed to enter his car and leaned back against his chair trying to make sense of what he had just witnessed.

"Aaron, let me explain." Bernard shouted as he ran towards Aaron's car in his boxers.

Aaron eyes widened and he turned the car on ignoring Bernard.

"Aaron!" Bernard called.

"Don't you dare mention my name again, you sick lunatic." Aaron said rolling up the car window to blur Bernard's words.

"If you don't want to die yet, get the fuck away from my car."

He started moving the car in warning while Bernard stepped back and watched as Aaron zoomed off.

Chapter 7

Ara sipped her coffee staring into space. It had been two weeks since she had sent Bernard out of the house and she hadn't heard from him. She couldn't blame him especially with the way she acted towards him that last time.

***

Bernard was still staring at Aaron's retreating car only to turn back when he heard a screeching sound.

Ara was dragging his luggage with her and when she saw him, she threw it at him.

It landed beside him with some of his clothes flying out and laying scattered on the floor.

"What is the meaning of this?" asked a Bewildered Aaron.

"I'm setting you free. You are now free to go back to your lover."

"You don't know what you are doing. You are not even thinking."

"How could you shift in front of him? How could you?" He was furious now.

"What about you? Were you thinking before you slept with a human? You know it's against the rules but you still did it."

"So by shifting in front of him, what were you planning to achieve?"

"I've achieved my aim. Let's see if he would want to have anything to do with you now."

He shook his head at her. "You are obviously not in your right senses so I'm going to leave you alone but I will be back."

***

Maybe she had overreacted but she couldn't blame herself totally. After seeing the scene in front of her that day, she couldn't think clearly and vented her anger the wrong way.

The doorbell rang interrupting her thoughts.

That must be Bernard. she thought as she placed her coffee on the table. He had texted her an hour ago that he was on his way to pick his things.

"Come in, the door is not locked."

The door opened to reveal a tired looking Bernard. His eyes were puffy as if he had been having a tough time sleeping.

"Are you ok?" she couldn't help but ask.

"What do you think?"

"Hey, don't give me an attitude," she warned.

"Or what? You have already done your worst. I've lost Aaron. He doesn't want to have anything to do with me. I haven't seen or heard from him in two weeks. Two weeks! Hope you are happy now?"

"Well don't blame me for trying to knock some sense into you." She was now standing up with her arms folded glaring at him.

"And why are you so mad? Is it because I cheated on you or because you just can't accept that the men you love don't want you?"

Her mouth hanged open in shock "What... what are you insinuating?"

He scoffed. "I'm not insinuating anything. He told me about your little romp in his office."

Seeing that she was confused, he continued, "I knew about his little crush on you, I just didn't know that you felt the same until he told me about what you guys did in his office. I must admit it did turn me on when he told me about it.”

He bit his lip on realising that he was being harsh on her.

“Ara,” he called softly. “I know I wronged you. I really did hurt you but believe me when I say I didn’t want to hurt you.”

“I couldn’t bring myself to tell you that I was in love with Aaron because I knew how much you loved me. I tried to break it off with him that was why he looked for me and came here,” he explained.

She sighed. “I’m sorry for overreacting. I shouldn’t have acted the way I did.”

“No.” Bernard shook his head. “You had every right to react that way.”

“No I don’t. I always told you that I would support you when you find your soul-mate but what did I do, I acted like a jealous lunatic and sent you away.”

She closed the space between them and asked. “Do you miss him?”

Bernard closed his eyes and smiled. “I do. I miss him so much,” he replied.

“I miss him, too,” she confessed while he opened his eyes in surprise.

“I didn’t plan on falling in love with him. It just happened that’s why I resigned because I couldn’t resist him. I feared that if I worked for him any longer I would cheat on you,” she explained.

He cupped her cheeks. “You did the right thing which I failed to do.”

“Shh...” she shushed him. “What would happen to us now?” she asked.

"It's left for you to decide."

She leaned her forehead against his. "I don't want to divorce you. I can't bring myself to let you go. Call me selfish but I can't."

"Then don't," he answered.

She gave him a questioning look. "What do you mean?"

"I totally understand. I get it. I don't want a divorce either."

"But what about Aaron?"

"As you can see he couldn't handle the truth and left me."

She looked away from him feeling guilty. She had let her anger get the best of her and now he was heartbroken.

"Let me make it up to you." She pressed her lips to his and he wrapped his hands around her waist pulling her closer. Her hands trailed down his chest to his groin and she rubbed him through his jeans earning a groan from him.

"What are you doing?" he asked taken aback by her actions.

"Shh... just imagine that I'm Aaron," she whispered.

That did the trick as he kissed her back harder making her lightheaded. His tongue parted her lips in search for hers as they twirled and danced like they always had.

They heard someone chuckle from behind them and turned to see Aaron leaning against the door.

"Am I interrupting something?" he asked. The door was slightly opened when he came so he didn't bother to knock. He just walked in to see such a beautiful sight.

"Aaron?" Bernard couldn't believe his eyes and rubbed at it to make sure he wasn't dreaming.

"The one and only." He smiled and moved away from the door spreading his arms out for a hug which Bernard obliged.

"I missed you so much." Bernard muttered, his voice almost breaking.

"I know. I missed you just as much," Aaron replied pulling away from Bernard a little bit and then capturing his lips. Their tongue swirled and sucked on each other before Bernard pulled away hazel eyes dark with desire.

"Why are you here? I thought you hated me."

"How could I hate you? I could never hate you. I just needed time to digest what happened. I did my research and learnt more about your kind. That was why I was away for those two weeks because I wanted to understand you."

"So you are not disgusted?"

"No, if anything I love you more than I ever had before."

Bernard's eyes watered. He couldn't believe his ears. Aaron still loved him. He still wanted him. It was a dream come true.

"Have you forgiven me? I mean I kept so many things from you," Bernard gazed at Aaron who shushed him.

"You are not the only one who keeps secrets. I totally understand you. Remember that nobody knows I'm bisexual not even my parents. So how could I not forgive you?"

Ara bit her lip as she watched the two men devour each other's lips. Seeing them dying to feel every inch of each other aroused her to no end but she knew she had to do the right thing.

She needed to leave and give them their privacy no matter how much she was dying to be wrapped in their arms. They didn't want her, they never did.

She made to leave and headed for the door but a hand grabbed her making her stop in her tracks. She turned to see that it was Aaron who was holding her back.

"Why are you leaving?" he asked.

"I don't want to be a third wheel," she replied.

Aaron smiled. "You are not a third wheel, Ara. You are the only woman I've ever fallen in love with."

She gulped. "You love me?"

"Yes I do. I have loved you from the moment I saw you step into my office. Why then should I let you go?"

He then turned to look at Bernard. "You are the only man I will ever love and she's the only woman I will ever love too. Is this ok with you?"

Bernard smiled cupping Aaron's cheek. "I'm perfectly ok with it as long as Ara is."

They both turned to look at Ara whose heart was beating frantically against her chest as she stared at the two loves of her life. This was a dream come true.

"Will you have us both?" Bernard asked.

Bernard was willing to share. There was nothing holding her back anymore.

"Yes," She shouted in joy and stripped out her night robe feeling Aaron's lustful gaze on her causing her clit to throb.

Aaron grabbed her by the waist and kissed her softly, his free hand gripping her ass making her moan against him.

She felt Bernard's presence behind Aaron sucking at his neck.

Aaron's hand reached up to cup her breast, squeezing it. His touch made her feel like she was on fire. She felt him grind his hardened length against her and that was when she knew there was no going back.

She pulled away and grabbed their hands and led them to her bedroom. She sat on the bed her legs spread waiting for them to take action.

She watched as Aaron stripped out of his trousers his eyes focused on her wet cunt.

For so long he had wanted this and here she was spread out in front of him on a platter of gold.

He grabbed each of her thigh and knelt between them. He ran his moist tongue over the edge of her lips teasingly making her gasp.

His tongue then began to thrust in and out of her dripping pussy eating her as if she was his last meal on earth.

She laid on her back, her legs buckling, "Oh god," she let out a loud moan.

She turned her head to the edge of the bed only to see Bernard watching them while stroking himself. She wondered when he had stripped.

Bernard smirked on catching her eyes on his cock and he climbed on the bed. He massaged her breasts, pinching her nipples with his fingers.

Aaron licked her faster and harder giving her no room to catch a breath. She grabbed unto Bernard's rigid cock and wrapped her lips around him causing him to throw his head back and groan in pleasure. She continued to suck on it watching his expression.

Aaron gave her three more hard strokes with his tongue and soon she was cumming. She grabbed unto Bernard's cock as she sucked him off.

Her screams her muffled by Bernard's cock as she felt the muscles of her entire body convulse.

Aaron withdrew from her thighs and stood up, unbuttoning his shirt as he looked down at her.

Bernard removed his cock from her mouth and pulled her by the hands to the bed. She was now fully laying down on the bed, legs spread with cum stained thighs.

She felt Aaron climb unto her, his thick manhood resting between her thighs and he leaned over and kissed her passionately. She wrapped her legs around his back ready for him to enter her.

He entered her gently yet forcefully causing her to scream out in pain and pleasure as he filled her completely.

She brushed her fingers through his hair as he withdrew from her slowly before slamming into her harder.

"Ahh" she groaned digging her nails into his shoulder as he sped up his pace, thrusting into her harder and faster. His thumb rubbed her throbbing clit making her yelp.

"Harder," she whispered gripping the bed spread but he didn't obey, he slowed down his pace and she looked up to see Bernard right behind him resting his hand on Aaron's ass.

The thought of what they were about to do turned her on the more.

Bernard pushed his cock slowly into Aaron's ass making the latter whip his head back.

Aaron continued to fuck her as Bernard entered him. It felt as if Bernard was fucking her too sending shivers down her spine.

Soon the room was filled with sounds of groans and slapping flesh.

The next thing she knew, she was trembling, climaxing and squirting as she spiraled into orgasm, screaming louder than she had ever had.

The two men increased their pace.

Aaron's real undoing was watching Ara orgasm.

He thrust into her hard and fast, exploding his seed into hers as his eyes rolled back into his head.

Bernard continued to fuck him harder and faster until he neared his orgasm. He grabbed unto Aaron's hips and pushed himself deep until he could take it no more and came into Aaron's ass.

Bernard pulled out his cock and collapsed beside a spent Ara. Aaron withdrew from her still sensitive body and collapsed at her other side.

She was now sandwiched in between the two men that she loved.

She kissed the two spent men on the lips feeling happier than ever because there was no place she would rather be than with them.

THE END